P9-CFI-836

by Alexis O'Neill
illustrated by
Laura Huliska-Beith
THE
RECESS
QUEEN
scholastic press new york

Library of Congress Cataloging-in-Publication Data
O'Neill, Alexis, 1949-
The Recess Queen / written by Alexis O'Neill;
illustrated by Laura Huliska-Beith.—1st ed. p. cm.
Summary: Mean Jean is the biggest bully on the school
playground until a new girl arrives and challenges Jean's
status as the Recess Queen.
ISBN 0-439-20637-5

[1. Bullies—Fiction. 2. Schools—Fiction.] I. Huliska-Beith, Laura, ill.
II. Title. PZ7.O5523 Re 2002 [E]—dc21 2001020841
12 11 10 9 8 7 6 5 4 3 2 1 02 03 04 05 06
Printed in Singapore 46
First edition, February 2002

The display type was set in Funhouse. The text type was set in 13-point Futura Bold.
The illustrations in this book were done in acrylics and collage.
Book design by Marijka Kostiw

Thanks to David who is always my first listener,
to my sister Donna, and
to all the kids who workshopped this story
with me at the following schools:
North Broad Street, Durhamville, Oneida Castle,
Seneca Street, Willard Prior, and H. W. Smith School.

MEAN JEAN was Recess Queen

and nobody said any different.

Nobody swung until Mean Jean swung.

Nobody kicked until Mean Jean kicked.

Nobody bounced until Mean Jean bounced.

If kids ever crossed her,

she'd push 'em and smoosh 'em,

lollapaloosh 'em,

hammer 'em, slammer 'em,

kitz and kajammer 'em.

the Art of SELF DEFENSE

"Say WHAT?" Mean Jean growled.

"Say WHO?" Mean Jean howled.

"Say YOU! Just who do you think you're talking to?"

Mean Jean always got her way.

UNTIL one day . . .

. . . a new kid came to school.

Katie Sue!

A teeny kid.

A tiny kid.

A kid you might scare

with a jump and a "Boo!"

But when the recess bell went ringity-ring,

this kid ran zingity-zing

for the playground gate.

Katie Sue SWUNG

before Mean Jean swung.

Katie Sue KICKED

before Mean Jean kicked.

Katie Sue BOUNCED

before Mean Jean bounced.

The kid you might scare with a jump

and a "BOO!"

was too new

to know about Mean Jean the Recess Queen.

Well, Mean Jean bullied through the playground crowd.
Like always, she pushed kids and smooshed kids,
lollapalooshed kids,
hammered 'em, slammered 'em,
kitz and kajammered 'em
as she charged after that Katie Sue.

CONFLICT
RESOLUTION

"Say WHAT?" she growled.

"Say WHO?" she howled.

"Say YOU!" she snarled and grabbed

Katie Sue by the collar.

"Nobody swings until Queen Jean swings.

Nobody kicks until Queen Jean kicks.

Nobody bounces until Queen Jean bounces,"

and she figured that would

set the record straight.

She figured wrong.

Katie Sue talked back!

Just as sassy as could be, she said,

"How DID you get so bossy?"

Then that puny thing

that loony thing,

grabbed the ball and

bounced away.

Oh! Katie Sue was one quick kid.

She bolted quick as lightning.

BOUNCITY BOUNCITY BOUNCE.

KICKITY KICKITY KICK.

SWINGITY SWINGITY SWING.

Mean Jean thundered close behind.

BOUNCITY

KICKITY

SWINGITY.

The Recess Queen was NOT amused.

She raced and chased and in-your-faced

that Katie Sue.

No one spoke.

No one moved.

No one BREATHED.

Then from her pack pulled Katie Sue

a jump rope clean and bright.

"Hey, Jeanie Beanie," sang Katie Sue.

"Let's try this jump rope out!"

Here's one thing true — until that day

no one DARED ask Mean Jean to play.

But that Katie Sue just hopped and jumped and skipped away.

"I like ice cream,

I like tea,

I want Jean to

jump with me!"

Jean just gaped and stared

as if too SCARED

to move at all.

So Katie Sue sang once more.

"I like popcorn,

I like tea,

I want Jean to

jump with me!"

Then from the side a kid called out,

"GO, JEAN, GO!"

And too surprised to even shout,

Jean jumped in with Katie Sue.

"I like cookies,

I like tea,

I want YOU to

jump with me!"

The rope whizzed and slapped,

FASTER,

FASTER,

the rope spun and flapped,

FASTER,

FASTER!

Till it caught in a tangled disaster.

But they just giggled and

JUMPED AGAIN!

WELL – now when recess rolls around

that playground's one great place.

At the school bell's ringity-ring

those two girls race zingity-zing

out the classroom door.

Jean doesn't push kids and smoosh kids,

lollapaloosh kids,

hammer 'em, slammer 'em,

kitz and kajammer 'em—

'cause she's having too much fun

rompity-romping with

her FRIENDS.

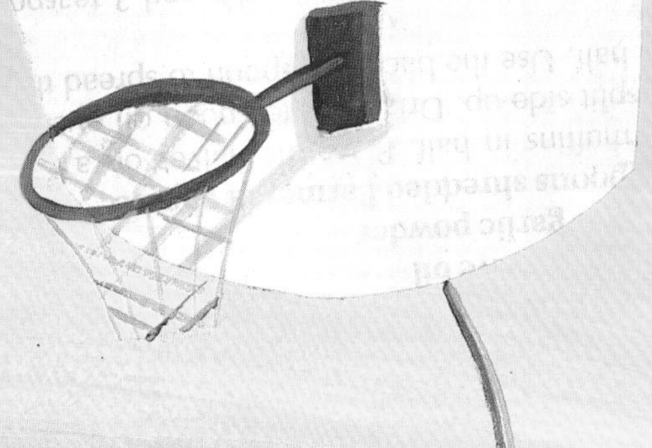

Bouncity, kickity, swingity,

Hoppity, skippity, jumpity,

Ringity, zingity,

YESSSSSS!

DISCARD